School Is Cool

tate publishing
CHILDREN'S DIVISION

Ruth Coates Diamond

This title is also available as a Tate Out Loud product. Visit www.tatepublishing.com for more information.

Published by Tate Publishing & Enterprises, LLC
127 E. Trade Center Terrace | Mustang, Oklahoma 73064 USA
1.888.361.9473 | www.tatepublishing.com

Tate Publishing is committed to excellence in the publishing industry. The company reflects the philosophy established by the founders, based on Psalm 68:11,
"The Lord gave the word and great was the company of those who published it."

Published in the United States of America
ISBN: 978-1-68164-141-6
1. Juvenile Fiction / School & Education
2. Juvenile Fiction / Poetry
15.06.23

"Josh, sweetie, wake up. It's time to go.
Today is your first day of school, you know."

Oh no! Oh no! What do I do?
Today is my very first day of school!

I pull the covers up over my head.
I really don't want to get out of bed!

My bed is a safe place, a place that I know.
School is scary, and I don't want to go.

I love my room, my toys, and my mom.
I'm trying so hard to try and stay calm.

When I'm in school, I will miss my cat.
Mom calls upstairs, "Don't forget your hat."

When I'm in school, who will read me
my books?
Mom calls to me, "Hang your clothes on
the hooks."

When I'm in school, I can't draw or paint.
Mom yells upstairs, "Hurry up, you'll be late."

When I'm in school, what will I eat?
Will I be cold, or will there be heat?

When I'm in school, I can't play outside.
I can't swing on my swings. I can't slide on
my slide.

When I'm in school, I can't play with
my friends.
I'll be so happy when this school day ends.

When I take my nap, I lay down my head.
I like to lie down on my own comfy bed.

When I'm in school, I can't play any games.
There are too many kids! Will I remember
their names?

Oh no! Oh no! What do I do?
Today is my very first day of school!

My stomach hurts, and I don't feel very well.
Mom says, "Hurry up, you'll miss the
first bell."

Maybe Mom will have pity if I shed a tear.
Mom calls, "Come down now, the bus will
be here."

Well, the tears didn't work, so here I go.
I'm off to school. Please, bus driver, go slow!

I walk through the door and into my class.
I just want to leave and run away fast.

I imagined my teacher is mean and a nag.
She is actually nice and hands me a bag.

The bag has folders, and pencils,
and books...
Some paper, some crayons, and some
erasers. Oh, look!

My teacher says "Hi" and "Welcome
to school."
Her name is Ms. Mitchell. She seems
pretty cool.

So far my first day has not been too tough.
In fact we are doing some very cool stuff.

In our class there are many books on
the shelf.
I'm learning to read so I can read to myself.

I'm learning to write and spell my name.
My teacher makes it fun, like playing a game.

I'm done with my book and carefully put
it away.
Then Ms. Mitchell says, "We have art
class today."

I paint a picture of my mom and dad.
I am having fun. School is not so bad.

My stomach is growling. I'm hungry for lunch.
We wash our hands, and I can't wait
to munch.

I fill my plate with good things to eat.
Some salad, some milk, and an apple,
how sweet.

I finish my lunch and turn in my tray.
Then Ms. Mitchell takes us outside to play.

We walk outside, and my eyes open wide.
There are plenty of swings and a long-
winding slide.

I've had so much fun, learned lots, made new friends.
I really don't want this school day to end.

"Come in," Ms. Mitchell calls, "It's time for a nap."
I walk to my cubby, and take out my mat.

I lie down so tired. I've been busy today.
I've had time to read, paint, eat, and play.

I've made new friends, and I remember their names.
There's Ricky, Lisa, Bryan, Kyle, Suzie, and James.

"Josh, sweetie, wake up. It's time to go.
Today is your second day of school you know."

I throw the covers off of my head.
I jump up and quickly get out of bed.

My bed is a safe place, a place that I know.
But school is not scary, and I can't wait
to go.

The End

e|LIVE

listen|imagine|view|experience

AUDIO BOOK DOWNLOAD INCLUDED WITH THIS BOOK!

In your hands you hold a complete digital entertainment package. In addition to the paper version, you receive a free download of the audio version of this book. Simply use the code listed below when visiting our website. Once downloaded to your computer, you can listen to the book through your computer's speakers, burn it to an audio CD or save the file to your portable music device (such as Apple's popular iPod) and listen on the go!

How to get your free audio book digital download:

1. Visit www.tatepublishing.com and click on the e|LIVE logo on the home page.
2. Enter the following coupon code:
   4ffd-eb77-5c51-17fa-22e7-a134-7445-84e1
3. Download the audio book from your e|LIVE digital locker and begin enjoying your new digital entertainment package today!